Tiger Flowers

Patricia Quinlan • pictures by Janet Wilson

Dial Books for Young Readers New York

Published by Dial Books for Young Readers
A Division of Penguin Books USA Inc.
375 Hudson Street
New York, New York 10014

Library of Congress Cataloging in Publication Data
Quinlan, Patricia.
Tiger flowers / by Patricia Quinlan ; pictures by Janet Wilson.—1st ed.
p. cm.
Summary: When his uncle, Michael, dies of AIDS,
Joel's dreams and thoughts of Michael keep his memory alive.
ISBN 0-8037-1407-6 (trade).—ISBN 0-8037-1408-4 (library)
[1. AIDS (Disease)—Fiction. 2. Death—Fiction.
3. Uncles—Fiction.] I. Wilson, Janet, 1952- ill. II. Title.
PZ7.Q4194Ti 1994 [E]—dc20 93-15214 CIP AC

The full-color artwork was prepared with watercolor
and casein. It was then scanner-separated and reproduced
in red, blue, yellow, and black halftones.

To my grandmother Dorothy Smith
and to the memory of my grandfather James Smith
P.Q.

For people with AIDS and those who care for them
J.W.

It was still dark when my sister Tara woke me up.

"When's Michael coming home, Joel?" she asked.

"I told you, Tara, Michael died," I said.

Tara's only three. She doesn't understand about dying.

Michael was my uncle. He was my mom's brother. I liked when he told us stories about when he and my mom were kids.

There's a tree house in our backyard. Michael helped me build it. He helped me nail the boards, and paint it. Michael told me that he had a tree house when he was the same age as me.

Underneath my tree house we have a garden with lots of flowers. Michael and I took care of them.

The tiger lilies were Michael's favorite. Tara calls them tiger flowers. Michael said he liked that name better.

Once, when Michael wasn't looking, I sprayed him with the garden hose. Michael pretended to be mad at me, but I knew he really wasn't.

Michael had a best friend named Peter. Michael, Peter, and I used to do things together. One day we went to a baseball game. We saw the Yankees play the Blue Jays. Peter bought me a baseball cap and a pennant that I taped to the wall beside my bed.

A few years ago Peter got sick. He had a disease called AIDS. Michael told me that when someone has AIDS, it's easy for them to get lots of other illnesses. Peter was sick for a long time and then he died.

Michael was very sad. He kept a picture of himself and Peter on the desk in his room. I saw him looking at it a lot. In the picture, Michael and Peter are standing in front of a model train set that Peter built. Sometimes when Michael took me to visit Peter, we would play with the train for the whole afternoon.

After Peter died, Michael got sick and came to live with us. He had AIDS too. Michael said that some of his friends didn't want to be with him anymore because he had AIDS. But he told me that I couldn't catch AIDS by being near him the way I caught the chicken pox from Tara.

When I got the chicken pox from Tara, Michael gave me a skateboard. After I got better, we made up a story about a boy who finds a magic skateboard that takes him anywhere he wants to go. We put the story in a book. Michael wrote the words and I drew the pictures. Often when I think about Michael, I like to read our book again.

Michael and I went to the zoo
once. The tiger was pacing back
and forth in his cage. "Tigers don't
belong in cages," Michael said.
"They want to run and be free."

When Michael got really sick,
my mom and I went to visit him
in the hospital. When we got there,
he was looking out the window.
He said that he just wanted to get
well enough to walk outside in the
sunshine again. While Michael was
talking to my mom, I drew a
picture of the tiger for him.

A few weeks after Michael died, I dreamed that Michael
and I were back at the zoo. We laughed a lot at the monkeys.

The zookeeper told us that the tiger had run away. When we got to the tiger cage, it was empty. "I'm free now too, like the tiger," Michael said.

I told my mom about my dream. "Michael loved you very much," she said. "I'm glad he's with you in your dreams."

I told my mom that sometimes when I think about Michael, I feel like I'm in a cold, lonely place inside me. "I feel that way too, Joel," she said. "It hurts a lot right now. After a while it will hurt less."

After Tara woke me, I couldn't sleep. I decided to go outside to my tree house. There was a cool breeze blowing as I walked through the garden.

When I was in my tree house, I thought about Michael. I felt like he was there with me. As I watched the sun come up on the tiger flowers, the cold place inside me got warmer.

After I climbed down, I heard Tara in the kitchen. I picked a tiger flower to give her.

"The tiger flowers were Michael's favorite, Tara," I said.
"They'll always be my favorite too."

CARVER CENTER